To all Black girls
— Shanice

To my beautiful niece, Laurie
— Kezna

Shanice Nicole is a Black feminist educator, facilitator, writer, and (out)spoken word artist. She believes that everyone has the power to make change and dreams of a freer world for us all.

Learn more about her work at shanicenicole.com.

Kezna Dalz is a multidisciplinary Black artist from Montreal. She cares about representation and portrays the beauty of womanhood, teenadult angst, and the worst of pop culture using vibrant colours.

You can find more of her work at teenadultt.com.

Author photo by Jackson Ezra

First edition
First printing - 2021
Printed in Canada by Marquis Book Printing
Distributed in Canada and the US by LitDistCo and in the UK and beyond by Turnaround Publisher Services

ISBN: 978-1-9990588-3-8 (hardcover)

Metonymy Press
PO Box 143 BP Saint Dominique
Montreal, QC H2S 3K6
Canada

We acknowledge the support of the Canada Council for the Arts.
Nous remercions le Conseil des arts du Canada de son soutien.

Canada Council
for the Arts

Conseil des arts
du Canada

Library and Archives Canada Cataloguing in Publication

Title: Dear Black girls / written by Shanice Nicole ; illustrations by Kezna Dalz.
Names: Nicole, Shanice, 1992- author. | Dalz, Kezna, 1996- illustrator.
Description: A poem.
Identifiers: Canadiana 20200223445 | ISBN 9781999058838 (hardcover)
Classification: LCC PS8627.I395 D43 2021 | DDC jC811/.6—dc23

DEAR BLACK GIRLS

WRITTEN BY SHANICE NICOLE

ILLUSTRATED BY KEZNA DALZ

METONYMY PRESS

Montreal, Quebec

Dear Black girls,

Yes, you, the ones who are starting something new
and wondering how you'll do
Yes, you, the ones who have big feelings
in your minds and bodies
Yes, you, the ones who are looking in the mirror
and wondering if you like what you see
Yes, you, the ones who are chasing
one of your many magical dreams.

Yes, you, Black girls. Yes, you.

Dear Black girls
all around the world,
this one is for you — for us.

Dear Black girls,
I love the way your Black skin
wraps itself around you,
as if it never wants to let go,
as if your colour is the richest thing
it has ever known.

Dear Black girls,
I love the way the kinks in your curls twirl,
bouncing and free,
afros worn like crowns,
with hair defying gravity

protected in locs and braids
and under wigs and weaves
because whatever you choose
is up to you, Queens.

And know that this goes
for the rest of your body
and anyone who tells you different
doesn't have to live, breathe, exist, be in it,

so please let it be known

that your body is your own

and only yours, dear Black girls.

Dear Black girls,
I love the way your forehead
takes up space on your face.
Strong, big, and wide,
like the oceans many of our ancestors survived —
hard, protecting the wonder that is your mind.

Dear Black girls,
I love the way your lips and mouths are full
as if they're already packed
with the stories you'll share
and the lessons you'll learn,
full as if they're already ready
for the battles you'll face
as you travel through time and space.

Ready to fight
and laugh
and kiss
and love
and scream

and everything else in between
you will have to do because
you are a Black girl in this world.

Dear Black girls,
I love the way your body curves,
like your Mama's and hers,
ancestry running through your veins,
reminding you each and every day
of who and what you come from.

The where isn't always clear
because the where isn't always known.
Our histories aren't always shown.
So many stories have been sewn,
pieced together and fabricated
and then used as a means of educating
little Black girls so that you grow up in this world
thinking you are not loved.

Thinking you are not everything.

But dear Black girls,
all around the world,
despite all you may feel, think, hear, or see,

know that you are honoured,
protected,
and loved . . .

. . . by Black girls like me.

Dear Black Girls,

Every single day I am reminded of how special Black girls are and of how lucky I am to be one. I originally wrote the poem "Dear Black Girls" in the summer of 2015 and dreamed of turning it into a children's book one day. I remember sharing that dream on a stage that summer and because I did, a friend connected me with a friend and the rest is history. So I want to remind you to always write and speak your dreams into existence. As Black girls we are often told that our dreams are not possible but know that they are. And so are you.

Kezna Dalz & Shanice Nicole

Dear Black Girls is a letter to all Black girls. No two Black girls are the same but we are all so very special. We come in different shapes, sizes, and shades. We are of different ages and have different abilities. We come from different countries and have different ethnic backgrounds. We speak different languages and believe in different spiritualities and religions. Our families look different and so do our friends. We define and embrace our own genders and sexualities. Everybody and every body is different but despite our differences, we all deserve to be loved just the way we are.

I hope you will read this book whenever you need a reminder of why Black girls are so special. I hope it will bring you joy and connect you with other Black girls all around the world. To be a Black girl is a true gift and I hope this book will help you treasure that forever.

Love always,

Shanice Nicole (February 2021)